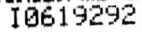

CLAIMED *by the* WOODSMAN

HALLIE BENNETT

BOOKS BY THIS AUTHOR

CHAPTER ONE

Sherry and Charis belt out "Girls Just Wanna Have Fun" at the top of their lungs from the raised stage in the back of the bar. Encouraging hoots and hollers cheer from the crowd, and I wonder how long I'm required to stay before sneaking back to my room. This weekend in the cute mountain town of High Ridge is all about Sherry's wedding on Sunday, but I'm not cut out for late nights spent drinking and partying.

I'd actually prefer spending more time on the hiking trails leading up the mountain. The refreshingly clean air and surrounding forests provide the perfect escape from the city and a beautiful bridal location. If it were my own wedding, I couldn't have chosen a better place.

Good thing marriage isn't in your future anymore.

Not after the five-year relationship with my ex ended last year—a relationship that lasted years longer than necessary since George traveled so much. With him gone most of the time, it was easy to let issues slide or forget them altogether.

We maintained separate homes, and it felt more like friends than lovers when we hung out—the physical aspect of our relationship lackluster. And when he'd finally admitted to never wanting to marry or have children? Well, that was the final nail in the coffin.

At thirty-two, my biological clock ticked like a time bomb. I couldn't afford to waste more years on someone whose plans for the future didn't match mine.

Studying the too-crowded bar as my friends start another karaoke song, my eye catches on a man sitting towards the back, his head thrown back in laughter, blonde waves glinting under the dim bar light. *Holy hell*. This mountain town had its fair share of attractive men based on all the guys I saw on our trip down Main Street earlier today, but this one tops the list.

Broad shoulders and muscled arms strained his tee while a five-o'clock shadow begged to be touched. Transfixed, I continue my perusal of the stranger and search for a companion. A man like him? I'd expect a pack of gorgeous women fluttering around, eager for attention. However, it seems like he's alone, and a brazen idea forms in my head.

I've never been the type for one-night stands, preferring the slow build of a relationship before jumping into bed. But what has my caution gotten me?

Absolutely nothing.

Except single and alone at my best friend's wedding—officially the last in our friend group who hasn't found love. Glancing around the room and spying on couples flirting or dancing increases my ire, envy becoming a green-eyed monster on my shoulder.

I want that.

The push and pull of attraction. Even if it's just for tonight.

My gaze wanders back to the blonde god, who's beginning to fuel a whole host of fantasies. Of wondering what's hiding under his tee... his jeans. Swallowing thickly at the image of firm muscles weighing heavily on my soft body, my thighs clench in need.

Wildly bad decisions are expected at bachelorette parties, right?

Tossing back a shot of the tequila sitting in front of me, salt from the rim clings to my lips, and I decide to go for it. The worst he can say is "No", which will sting, but it's not like I'll have to see him again. Shuffling to my feet, courage and fear roil around in my stomach, mixing with the alcohol coursing through my veins.

My usual routine when it comes to hot men is to avoid them out of insecurity. A woman of average beauty and more than a few extra pounds rounding my waist, their attractiveness naturally outshines mine and makes me feel uncomfortable, since I know they'd never be interested in me romantically. But tonight's all about risk. I'm sick of feeling like an outcast in the sea of happy couples I'm surrounded by and want to experience—just once—a night of passion with the sexiest man I've ever seen.

Sliding next to the stranger, my hands slap the counter in excitement, causing the man to jump at my sudden appearance.

Calm down. Don't scare him away by being overeager.

"Need something, darlin'?" His rich, velvety voice sizzles over my skin, blazing a path to my contracting sex.

That's never happened before...

Sex with George had been perfunctory. He'd never elicited such a reaction as this man did with three words. Imagining what else he could wring from my aroused body, my gaze drops to his mouth, then lower to the large hand wrapped around his beer bottle.

He has to agree to sleep with you first.

"I'm Kate. I'm here for my friend's bachelorette party." *And I want you to fuck me.* Pointing to Sherry on the stage, my mind scrambles for a better way to voice my desire. He follows the gesture before returning amused eyes back to me.

"Name's Micah." He tips his bottle towards the performance. "Why aren't you up there with them?"

"Trust me, I'm doing everyone a favor by not singing." A self-deprecating laugh burst out, remembering an ill-fated talent show in sixth grade. I'd never subject myself to that sort of humiliation again. Inhaling a steadying breath, I take the plunge and say, "Actually, I thought we could—"

"There you are! I've been looking for you!" A beautiful woman with long raven hair wraps an arm around Micah's shoulder, and mortification sweeps through me as ice water extinguishes my brief bout of bravery. No wonder he sat alone. He was waiting on his date to arrive—not some desperate bachelorette to proposition him. A bachelorette who couldn't hold a candle to the beautiful model pressed against him.

"I'm sorry, I didn't realize... Nevermind, it doesn't matter. Have a good night." Awkwardly backing away from the scene, I turn tail and run, needing to escape the suddenly stifling bar. At least the woman appeared before I completely humiliated myself—a paltry silver lining.

Pushing through the crowd of people, a bright "Exit" sign beckons above a rear door. I shove the heavy metal door open before stumbling into a dark alley as a welcome breeze cools the nervous sweat gathered on my forehead. A derisive chuckle echoes off the brick buildings I'm sandwiched between.

Of course, the one time I step out of my comfort zone—try to take a risk—I fall flat on my face. All the wedding festivities must have addled my brain to think I could pull off a one-night stand with a sexy stranger. Best to stick with the Georges of the world—safe and predictable with a slow build-up.

And boring. The knowledge taunts me, and my staid future looms ahead.

Ready to go to bed and forget the past fifteen minutes, I text Sherry to let her know I'm returning to my room, so she doesn't worry about my disappearance. After the wedding will be soon enough to fill her in on tonight's mistake. If I even bother to tell her. While she'll praise my courage, it'll only serve as another reminder of my embarrassing failure.

Leaning against the wall for support, head tapping lightly on the brick, I allow myself a moment to calm down when the squeak of door hinges draws my attention.

"Kate? Are you okay?"

My back straightens at the familiar voice, and surprise beats in my chest, a timpani chorus banging to life. Why did he follow me out here?

"Yes, of course. I'm sorry again for crashing your date. I didn't mean to interrupt."

Shadows play over his high cheekbones before he steps closer, forehead wrinkled in confusion. "Date? You mean Lindsey? She's just a friend."

"Oh." The simple word falls between us, but I'm not sure how else to respond. They seemed like pretty close friends if she felt comfortable enough to drape her slim body over his larger one.

Micah jerks a thumb towards the bar where dull music thuds through the walls. "You looked like a woman with a plan inside, and being the obliging type of man I am, I thought I'd check to see if I could help. Feel free to tell me to take a hike if I read the situation wrong." A boyish grin of mischief lights up his face as mine heats at having such obvious intentions.

"And you're just a little cocky, too, huh?"

He puts a hand over his heart, intimating a wounded stance. "Now, darlin', that hurts. *Little* wouldn't be the way I'd describe it." An exaggerated wiggle of his light brows follows, and I laugh, buoyed by his flirting.

"You're trouble."

"True. Ask anyone in High Ridge. But I can make it worth your while, if that's what you want." An inquisitive examination follows as his gaze drinks in my body from head to toe. Squirming under his inspection, I grasp at the former stings of my courage, reviving them from the brink of death at the abrupt change of circumstances.

Here's your opportunity to accept a walk on the wild side. Say yes!

"Right here?"

His forehead crinkles in astonishment, and even I'm shocked by the suggestion. Sex in an alley behind the bar? Not romantic or responsible. More like dirty and hot.

Which is exactly what you need.

"Wherever you want. It's your decision." Micah moves closer, his arms caging me in. Spicy cologne overrides the faint musty smell of the alley, wrapping me in an intoxicating cloud of his scent.

"I want you here. Now." *Before fear or common sense rushes in to change my mind.*

"A woman after my own heart," he murmurs, brushing his lips over mine—a prelude to what's coming. Rough palms skim over my hips until he reaches the hem of my navy sundress. "And so conveniently prepared. Was this part of your plan all along? Night on the town with your girls before seducing some lucky man into fucking this wet cunt? Glad I made the cut."

Oh god, so am I.

Any chance of a coherent response evaporates. No one has ever spoken to me this way, and I don't know how to handle it except for enthusiastically returning his kiss with everything I've got. Tugging roughly on his blonde hair, our mouths meet again in a frenzied embrace while his fingers slip under the hem of my dress to rest against the soaked center of my panties.

I can't believe how aroused I am. I literally saw Micah and exchanged a few sentences. Nothing spectacular, yet there's an ache in my core, a readying for his touch.

Perhaps I needed this more than I thought.

Forging my own exploratory path, one hand scrambles under his tee to find hard muscles rippling along a taut stomach—a marked difference from my past sexual exploits—and a frisson of insecurity slinks through my desire.

Nothing about me is fit or firm. I like sweet treats and knitting while watching Hallmark movies.

Damn, I sound like a grandma.

Except grandmas don't usually fuck strangers behind bars...

The thought reignites my confidence; I'm young—in the prime of my life. So what if I'm curvier than he might be used to?

By the way his burgeoning cock is digging into my hip, I don't think he minds.

"It was either you or the man at the end of the bar dressed in leather," I quip, finally able to form some kind of response to his earlier comment.

"Harold? I heard he's got an extra toe on his right foot and smells like sour milk." The ridiculous description makes me giggle, something I've never done during sex, and it's an odd combination—this mix of lust and laughter.

"An extra toe sounds interesting..."

Micah surges past the cotton barrier of my panties to plunge deep into my pussy, palm slapping my clit. The swift move draws a yelp of surprise before I settle into the rough stroke of his fingers. Forget slow build-up. This was a dominant display of his control over me.

"You got a secret foot fetish I should know about?" he grunts, increasing the rapid pace of his thrusting.

A swell of endorphins runs beneath my skin as an orgasm builds, making it harder to concentrate on flirty banter. This may be the fastest a man's made me come, a fact Micah would love to hear, I'm sure. An air of assurance emanates from him; he knows he's skilled. But the arrogance doesn't bother me, especially when I'm on the receiving end of his particular talents.

"A lady never reveals all of her secrets."

"But she'll come on my hand before soaking my dick? Is that how the saying goes?" The teasing taunt goes unanswered as my body finally peaks—legs turning to jelly—the force of Micah's weight on mine the only thing keeping me upright.

A steep crash of fatigue threatens after such an intense spike of pleasure.

Don't wimp out now or you'll miss the main attraction.

Right. He still hasn't properly fucked me yet. And like a rubber band, I bounce back into awareness; I definitely don't want to miss that.

CHAPTER TWO

MICAH

D*amn, am I one lucky son of a bitch.*

Something my older brother Rhett never failed to remind me of, but as the angel to his devil according to the people of High Ridge, I can't help it. Outgoing and personable, I'm the direct opposite of Rhett, and those traits serve us well in a town that's looked down on the Olson boys all of our lives. Despite the gossip following our family, my charm sways business our way and is a major factor in the success of the lumber and construction company I co-own with my brother and our friend, Asa.

The three of us grew up on the wrong side of town, a fact that sticks with you in a small community. Add in Rhett and Asa's dark looks and standoffish attitudes, and you've got a recipe for the quintessential black sheep of High Ridge—a title not conducive to building a successful business. Which is why my role with the company is so important.

I even closed on another logging contract this afternoon, prompting my need to celebrate at Hank's Bar. Unfortunately, Asa had been too eager to get back to his woman, Poppy, and Rhett hardly ever left his cabin on Black Mountain after work hours. But I never let their hermit tendencies stop me from having a good time.

And thank god, I didn't tonight or else I wouldn't have this sexy as fuck woman panting in my ear after her orgasm.

When Kate approached me at the bar, my dick had immediately stood to attention, twitching in response to the tits threatening to spill over the top of her dress. A shy hunger burned in her eyes, and I recognized a sensual need matching my own. Then, Lindsey showed up, a bucket of snow dousing the flames as Kate skittered away like a scared rabbit.

But you caught her in the end.

Her pussy flutters around my fingers as if to remind me of my good fortune, and a thrum of satisfaction pounds in my chest—pleasing Kate paramount. She's lassoed me with a rope twined with lush curves, demure smiles, and cute banter. Wouldn't Rhett find the comparison fitting, since he's always likening me to a young buck, roaming wild and free?

I can't even explain how she did it. From one minute to the next, I was hooked with no rhyme or reason. Braced between me and the brick building, lethargy outlines her relaxed posture as my mind works to figure out the puzzle of Kate's tether.

You really want to focus on this conundrum when you could be feeling her writhing on your dick?

Good point.

Hovering over the button of my jeans, I brush a kiss over her ear before asking, "Are you ready for more, darlin'?"

"Yeah, I'm good. Just needed a quick breather." She musters enough energy to tilt her hips in an effort to reach my swollen erection, and it's all the confirmation I need to continue. Pulling out my wallet, I grab the condom tucked in the center pocket before stuffing the leather billfold back to its original position.

The foil wrapper crackles in the night as I tear it open and quickly cover my cock, and Kate releases a bemused chuckle. "You always keep one of those on hand? Should I be worried?"

Chagrin streaks to the forefront, but I shrug it off. "I like to be prepared, and I'm clean as a whistle. You?"

"Same. I haven't had sex in—" She abruptly stops, eyes lifting to a point over my shoulder. "It doesn't matter. We're safe. We're good. Proceed, please."

She has a quirky way of speaking sometimes, but I find it adorable. "As my lady commands." Grinning, my body shifts forward, cock sliding through slick folds until I press against her tight opening. Our location dictates a hard and furious pace prior to someone accidentally stumbling onto our precarious positions, but I slowly ease inside first, making sure she's comfortable before going balls to the wall.

Literally.

My amused gaze glances at the red brick behind Kate's head, strands of her hair stuck to the scratchy stone. When I'm convinced she's still with me—fully on board with the rough fuck coming her way—my restraint lets loose with a rumble of excitement.

Hips pistoning deep, the slap of our bodies resounds in the dark alley, and Kate's tits bounce with every thrust—a delicious treat calling my name. One hand reaches to stretch her dress's thin cotton neckline until it rests under her breasts, propelling the perky tips high. A gasp jolts through Kate as my lips latch onto a rosy nipple, teeth gently holding the sensitive peak in place for quick lashes of my tongue.

"Micah..." Her nails scrape along my scalp, and the slight pain causes me to nip more forcefully in retribution. She repeats my name, but this time it's high-pitched as her back arches, pussy clamping down on my tunneling dick.

Fuck, my girl liked that.

Wait. My girl?

I'm not Asa who found his woman stranded on the side of the road and kept her as his. This is a fling. She's here for a wedding and will leave soon. It can't be more than tonight.

But the thought weighs on me, not feeling right, which makes little sense. While I'm not opposed to settling down, I've enjoyed living for the moment and staying free as a bird. My string of women, as Rhett refers to them, always know the score and want the same thing—to have fun, no commitment. Now, my previous desire for hook-ups rings hollow when I think of Kate, and I don't have a clue why.

Stop thinking so hard, dammit. You've got a curvy little package deserving your attention.

"God, you feel so good." The mumbled admission interrupts my confused musings and reinforces the reminder to focus on what matters—fucking Kate so well her screams of ecstasy echo in the alley. Fucking her so well she might consider seeing me again, giving me a chance to figure out what's going on in my head and heart.

Now, there's a solid plan.

Voices drift from the front of the bar, and the threat of discovery pushes me to redouble my efforts, delving deep and grinding against her clit until the silky walls of her cunt convulse around me, forcing my explosive orgasm to follow hers. I muffle her cry of bliss with a greedy kiss, tasting tequila on her tongue.

It's earthy with a hint of sweet—the perfect description of the goddess in my arms.

Reluctantly easing away after waiting for us to catch our breaths, I remove the used condom, tying it off before tossing it in a bin a few feet away.

"How are you feeling?" I ask, helping her readjust the displaced dress.

"Tired, but in a good way. Thank you for—" Piercing chimes emanate from a pocket on her dress, and Kate pauses, an apologetic expression clouding her face. "I'm sorry. I'm not sure who'd be calling me at this time..." She checks the name on the screen and frowns. "It's my friend, the bride. I should probably answer."

Nodding, I step back to give her some space. "Go ahead. No worries." My retreat allows me a moment to observe her unencumbered. Dark flushes of color stain her skin from the scratch of my night beard, and the single-minded temptation to lick and soothe the marks rears strongly in my limbs.

A rapid conversation with hysterical crying blares from the phone, halting the purposeful step I'd made towards Kate. *Christ, I'm being reeled in without her even trying!*

"Everything will work out. I'm heading back now." Hanging up, she runs an agitated hand through spiraling curls, mussing the untamed strands even more. "Apparently, all of Sherry's drinking tonight has culminated in a serious case of cold feet, so I'm needed to remind her exactly why she's marrying her fiance."

"Sounds fun. Do you need a ride?" *Say "yes".*

"I planned on walking, since we're at the bed-and-breakfast down the street, but a ride would be nice. Thank you." We walk side by side out of the alley as if nothing out of the ordinary happened—as if we didn't just fuck like a pair of horny bunnies.

My truck's parked on the other side of the road, and it's not five minutes later that I'm pulling up in front of The Timber Bed & Breakfast. Shifting to park, I hurry around to the passenger side and help Kate down from the high cab.

Awkwardness pervades the air before a determined exhale bursts from her. "I guess this is goodbye. Thanks again for the ride and for the... um, you know." She waves a vague hand in the air to encompass our passionate joining. The gesture shouldn't be so endearing, but a persistent warmth puddles in my stomach at the shy movement.

"Sex? Orgasms? Can you be a little more specific?" I tease, tugging on the bow decorating the center of her dress. If only we'd had enough time to let me tug the whole fucking outfit off; I would've loved to see the rounded hills and valleys of her body on full display.

"All the above." Kate laughs, and the infectious sound makes me want to haul her close again for a kiss—to capture her joy.

Not going to happen. Just let her go. Remember what this is.

A growing pit in my heart sits like a lead weight, starting from the center and bleeding outward, until I figure "Fuck it" and decide to take my chances. "Maybe we could—"

"Kate, where have you been? Sherry is freaking the fuck out, and we need you now!" A petite woman shouts from the entryway, light pouring into the night, and the moment's lost.

"I'm sorry. I've got to go, but it was nice meeting you! Bye!" Regret mars her features as Kate jogs away, shooing her friend inside after a last wave of farewell.

My body stays frozen to the sidewalk, staring at the quaint house doubling as a B&B. The Pattersons had our company refinish the hardwood floors two years ago, and I picture Kate scurrying through those halls on a mission to help her friend.

Sighing in resignation, I force thoughts of her curvy body and sweet personality out of mind as I start the journey home. Whatever came over me tonight—the need for more than a one time hook-up—will surely pass by morning, and I'll probably be thankful we were interrupted before asking to hang out again.

Sure, keep telling yourself that.

CHAPTER THREE

KATE

PRESENT TIME

Groups of men work purposefully around the lumberyard of Olson-Keller Lumber & Construction, a place I never imagined frequenting. Yet, one passionate night months ago changed the course of my life irrevocably.

An understatement.

Gathering my courage before approaching the man partially responsible for my predicament, a rueful chuckle chafes my throat. Of course, the ultimate reason for ending my relationship with George last year was marriage and children only for an impulsive hook-up to result in a surprise pregnancy.

Life loves ironic twists.

Rubbing sweaty palms down my jeans one more time, I exit the car and head towards a large building at the center of the lumberyard, praying Micah's here today. His potential reaction to my news is a complete mystery to me, and the unknown sets my equilibrium off-kilter. We're strangers; we didn't plan for this to happen. Could I blame him if he refused to take part in our child's life?

It would certainly put a dent in the fantasy you've created in your head of a future where the two of you are together and in love. A silly dream, really. I'd struggled to get him out of my mind after our interlude, but when I'd discovered my pregnancy? All those wishes for family—a caring husband and a precious baby—stampeded in like a damned herd of horses, vying for supremacy.

Various desks litter the office space once I'm inside, and a woman sitting up front greets me with a smile.

"Hi, may I help you?"

"I'm looking for Micah." No last name. The only reason I know he works here is because I remember the logo on the side of his truck when he dropped me off at the B&B.

"Do you have an appointment?"

"No, but I won't be long. Five minutes tops." An optimistic estimate by my account, but I need the receptionist to let me see Micah.

Skepticism clouds the woman's face, and I wonder how often random women show up here searching for him. *Probably more than you'd like.* The image doesn't sit well, and my stomach is already rolling with nerves and baby hormones.

"Please." The slight desperation in my voice must sway her because she motions for me to take a seat and picks up a phone, presumably to call him.

Long minutes later, Micah strolls into the building, and those blasted hormones shoot off again at how attractive he is. A part of me wondered if I'd imagined the powerful effect he had on me, but, apparently, I didn't because my body still has a visceral reaction to his.

Who knew I had a thing for lumberjacks? I thought as the sight of his dark jeans, boots, and gray plaid shirt elicited a pulse of need.

"Kate." He sounds happy to see me, his gaze drinking in my body and an expression I don't recognize crosses his face. "Let's step outside for some privacy."

Micah motions me forward, holding the door open, as cool air sweeps over us. It's fall in the mountains. Soon it'll be Thanksgiving, then Christmas, and I can't help but imagine how beautiful the holidays must be on the mountain when it's covered in snow.

Picture perfect for a cozy family photo.

"I'm sorry to show up unannounced, but I thought in-person would be better than a phone call." Avoiding the soft question in his eyes and eager to get it over with, I blurt out, "I'm pregnant, and the baby is yours."

Distant sawing cuts through the silence after the explosive piece of news. I wrap my cardigan tighter around me, forming a much-needed self-hug, as I await his judgment. This conversation has been weighing on me ever since the pregnancy test came back positive, but I'd underestimated how much stress centered on his response. Because, however ready I am to be a single mom, I'd like our baby to at least know their father.

Don't kid yourself: you'd like a lot more than knowing *him, too.*

"How long have you known? It's been four months, Kate, and you're just now telling me?" The notes of frustration and unexpected hurt in his voice whips at my frayed nerves. I hadn't expected the timeline of learning about my pregnancy to upset him more than the actual baby.

"The first trimester needed to pass safely. It didn't seem necessary to worry you until things were more... settled." A cowardly move on my part perhaps, but I've always been cautious, protecting myself. The truth is, he was the first person I wanted to call; I longed for him to ride in like a knight in shining armor.

But it wasn't fair to expect that from him. He'd signed on for a one time affair, not a lifetime of commitment.

Micah paces back and forth, agitation written in his tense movements. Focusing on the mountain standing tall behind him, the serene landscape helps ground me as tears blur my vision. *Dammit*. Normally, I appreciate the catharsis of a good cry, but now is not the time.

"So, I never would've known," he mutters to himself. "*Christ!*" Micah runs a hand through his hair, and another huff of disgruntlement explodes from his chest. "If you—" He stops short, facing me, a cloud of concern washing away the anger. "Please don't cry, darlin'. I'm sorry for blowing up; it's just upsetting thinking of you going through something as terrible as a miscarriage alone. I'd want to be there for you."

The kind sentiment brings forth another slew of tears. He can't be this good. This can't be real.

"But the past doesn't matter. Our future does, and we're having a baby."

Strong arms encircle my expanded waist, and I grant myself permission to rely on him for the time being, head resting on his firm chest. "I apologize for crying. Unfortunately, it happens a lot these days. And if I made the wrong decision not to tell you earlier, then I'm sorry for that, too. This has all been so much, and I don't know what I'm doing half the time, and I..."

"Shh, it's okay. You're not doing this alone anymore. We'll figure things out together from now on."

A shudder of relief courses down my spine at his promise. *Don't get too comfortable. This can't last forever.*

CHAPTER FOUR

MICAH

My mind races with a list of things to do before the baby arrives: move Kate in with me, get married, set up a nursery... Because I'm going to be a dad and a husband. *Holy fuck.*

She hasn't said "yes" yet, pal.

The prospect of becoming a father and husband so soon should scare me, but I've been dreaming about Kate since the night we went our separate ways. That magnetic force I'd felt pulling me towards her hadn't diminished over time—only magnified. Hell, it'd grown so much in those few hours after our tryst that I'd driven to the B&B in search of Kate the next day, only to discover the wedding party had left, and the concierge wouldn't share their private information.

No matter how thick I laid on the charm or pushed my connection to the owners through past renovations. Now, fate's deemed fit to bring Kate back to me, and I won't screw it up this time around.

I'm going to tie her to me by any means necessary. Knocking her up is a great, though unplanned, start.

A watery shiver reminds me to focus on the present moment, which means make the crying pregnant woman in my arms feel better. "This might be jumping the gun, but what do you think about naming the baby Harold?"

A choking sputter of disbelief ripples over her. "What? Harold?"

"It seems fitting, considering his presence at the bar the night we met. Because of him, you chose me instead, and look where we are now."

"We are not naming our child after an extra-toed bar dweller. That's where I draw the line." An amused chuckle brings a tiny grin to Kate's face as she wipes away stray tears with my help. The wet shine in her eyes illuminates the pools of blue to an even brighter hue—a mesmerizing sight I can't look away from.

"Sounds like you have pretty strong feelings on the subject of Harold. Does that mean he's not invited to the wedding?"

"Wedding?"

Uh-oh. Shouldn't have mentioned it so soon.

Fumbling for words, I scratch the back of my neck. "Well, yeah. This wasn't what I had in mind as far as a proposal, but I definitely want to marry you."

The deer in headlights expression emanating from her would be comical if it wasn't so damn important she agreed to stay with me.

"You barely know me. You don't want to marry me." She shifts back, adding space between our bodies, and I immediately miss her soft warmth. "A baby doesn't necessitate marriage these days. This isn't the nineteen fifties."

"No, but I want our child to have my name." My voice drops lower as I cup her jaw, guiding her face back to mine, so she can read how serious I am. "And I need you bound to me, so I don't lose you again."

I catch a brief glimpse of yearning before it disappears, her eyes rolling heavenward. Maybe I imagined that look of agreement. *Or it was a glint of sunlight.*

"You didn't lose me. We parted after a mutually satisfactory one. Night. Stand." She emphasizes each word as if I don't remember what that night was supposed to be. "Typical behavior after such nights."

"For other people, yes. But not for us. A fucking boulder sat in my gut all evening after leaving you, but when I returned to the B&B the next day, you were already gone."

"You came back for me?" A light breeze sends a tendril of amber whispering across her cheek. Brushing the wayward strand off Kate's heart-shaped face, I keep my hold on her so she can't look away.

"Yes. Hell, I didn't want to leave you in the first place, but I let my head rule. Let it tell me that my feelings would pass. That my intense need for you was irrational. Too quick. But I don't care about any of that anymore. Screw what's reasonable."

"Micah, what are you doing out here? Aren't you supposed to be with Tom over at Jensen's? We don't have time for you to fuck around with one of your women." My brother Rhett's rough voice cuts through air, and I'm tempted to pop him in the jaw for the interruption.

"One of your women?" Kate questions, her nose crinkling in concern.

And for that comment, too.

"Ignore my brother. He's just being an ass." I glare at Rhett before answering. "Tom will be fine on his own. There's a personal matter with Kate that needs handling first." My hand gestures between them as an introduction. "Rhett, Kate."

Rhett nods in her direction and waves me closer for some privacy. Apologizing for the rude intrusion, I trot over to my brother, though I'm careful to monitor Kate because I'm half afraid she'll bolt.

Rhett's hands bulge in the pockets of his coat, tight fists clenching and releasing as he tries to maintain his temper. "What kind of personal matter do you need to deal with in the middle of a workday? This is a place of business. You can try remembering that the next time a woman of yours wants to visit."

Gritting my teeth at his condescending tone, the urge to knock him down a peg grows. This wasn't some woman off the street. Someone I'd fucked and forgot about. This was Kate. The mother of my child.

He could assume the worst of me—I suppose I've earned it—but not her. There's no comparison between her and past women I've dated.

"Watch it. She'll be joining our family soon, so you better start making a better impression."

"Joining our family?" Rhett asks incredulously. "What the hell are you talking about?"

"She's pregnant, and the baby's mine."

A skeptical brow scrunches his forehead. "How can you be sure? Have you done a paternity test?"

"No," I growl in warning, "and I don't need to. It's mine. Don't suggest otherwise again."

"Micah, come on. Be smart about this. You can't know this woman well," Rhett argues, righteousness radiating off him like dust from a chainsaw. "You haven't mentioned anything about her, but now you're willing to take on fatherhood without proof to support her claims of your paternity?"

Damn right.

Scrubbing a weary hand down my face, I sigh—emotions warring inside my gut. Frustration because I don't like the insult to Kate's character or my judgment. But also understanding because he's my big brother, and he's always worried about me and my wild antics.

"We don't share every detail of our lives, you know. Kate's important to me, and I trust her. So, believe me when I say the baby's mine, and she's going to be my wife." *As soon as I get her to agree to my proposal.*

Rhett shakes his head, disappointment weighing down his shoulders. "You've always done what you wanted. God knows I can't stop you. I just hope for your sake you're making the right decision." A resigned frown tightens his mouth before he adds quietly, "But whatever happens, you'll always have me."

"Thanks, bro." We don't discuss our feelings a lot, mostly because Rhett's a fucking locked box, but times like these remind me how fortunate I am to have him. "Now, can I get back to my woman? It can't be good for her to be standing around on her feet this long, at four months pregnant."

"Your woman," he mutters. "Fuck. You and Asa with the caveman shit."

"Don't think you won't be the same way when you find your girl," I tease, knowing how obsessed Rhett can get about certain subjects. The woman who snares his attention will be in for one possessive caveman of her own.

"Forget it. I'm destined to be alone, and that's the way I like it."

Whatever you say, brother.

Hurrying back to Kate, I notice a sharp tremor wrack her body despite the jacket she's wearing. As nice as the cooler weather is, we need to get some place warm and private. Besides, Rhett has a point about the lumberyard being our business.

Not that I care if people know Kate's mine, but they don't need to hear our intimate conversations and share them with everyone in town. "Want to head to my place? We'll be able to talk more freely there, and you can warm up."

She nods, bouncing on her toes in eagerness. "Sounds good. I'll follow you in my car."

Grateful for her easy compliance, I head toward my truck and brace for the talk ahead. A discussion designed to seal our future—one way or the other.

CHAPTER FIVE

KATE

Micah's house surprises me as we stop in front of a cute, tiny home. Made of logs standing at two levels, windows line one whole side of the miniature cabin look-alike.

"You live here?" I ask, appreciating the efficiency of a tiny home but not seeing how it'll work for a baby.

You're not really going to marry him. Or live with him. What's it matter?

I'm shocked his first suggestion was marriage after learning about the baby, and like a schoolgirl with her head in the clouds, the urge to accept his proposal—to believe in fairytale endings—simmers beneath the cloak of reality.

"Yep. I know it's different, but it's hand-built by me, Rhett, and our friend Asa. A few years ago, when the tiny house trend exploded, we dipped our toes in creating our own versions to sell. Eventually, I decided I wanted to give it a try, too, so here we are." He shrugs like it's not a big deal, but I'm impressed he's lasted so long in such a small space.

Well, he is only one man.

We walk past a fire pit before Micah opens the front door and motions me inside. As expected, a rustic vibe permeates the space—leather seats, framed pictures of mountains, and quirky animal statues peeking out of hiding spots.

"Would you like something to drink?"

"Water, please. And..." I pause, embarrassed. "Could I use your bathroom? My bladder isn't what it used to be with this little one pressing on it."

"Of course! Sorry, I should've thought of that. It's through here." He slides a pocket door to reveal a small toilet and shower—the sink located directly below the showerhead. Nothing marked the floor to separate the different areas, and a part of me balked at the set-up.

Get over it. Do your business and get out.

After a hasty few minutes, I find Micah arranging a pull-out table and two foldable chairs. Glasses of water sit on the worn wooden top, light from the windows reflecting prisms of color.

Micah waits for me to sit down before settling in his own seat, and my stupid heart clutches at his chivalrous manner. *Stay strong, girl.* Clasping sweaty hands together, I rest them on the table and prepare for our upcoming discussion.

Starting with an easy question, I ask, "First things first, after your reaction earlier, I assume you want to be a part of the child's life?"

"Damn right. I want us to be a proper family: you, me, and the baby."

"And by proper, you mean husband and wife?"

His jaw tightens in a brisk nod. "We may live in modern times, but I confess to being old-fashioned when it comes to you. In fact, I feel positively primeval." A heated cloud descends over his eyes, warming the rich amber color. My hormones act up again with an excited twitch as my nipples bud into hard peaks. "I want you legally bound to me."

Bound to him.

Flustered sparks cascade through my veins at his declaration, and inappropriate visions of my body laid out before him, restrained by silk ties, instill a whole other meaning to his words. Breathing deeply, the spiciness of his cologne doesn't help matters.

"But I can't marry a man I barely know, even if he is the father of my child." Resolve struggles under the onslaught of arousal, and I'm a little angry at my body's betrayal during such an important talk. I need to keep wits about me, not succumb to desire. "We could be terrible together, and I'd prefer not to put my kid through a divorce." My mind flashes to the messy separation between my own parents, and a vow to protect my own child from such distress echoes in my head.

"Agreed about the divorce part. The stranger part we can rectify. High Ridge is my hometown, though being local didn't endear the townspeople to our family. We lived on the outskirts of town and tended to get in a lot of trouble. I graduated from UNC with a degree in business, specializing in project management." He ticks off facts with his fingers before concluding with a cheeky smile. "Oh, and I'll turn twenty-seven in December, so the entire month gets dedicated to presents for me."

"You're only twenty-six?" Discomfiture makes me fidget in my seat. He's six years younger than me! Which isn't illegal or really even that outlandish, but it never occurred to me to ask about his age.

"Why? How old are you?"

"Thirty-two."

A sly grin eases across his mouth as he inspects me from head to toe—or at least as much of me as he can see with a table in the way. "Hmm... An older woman. I like it."

"You make me sound like a cougar. I'm not that old." A reluctant chuckle bubbles up, my thighs rubbing together at the implied taboo of a relationship between us. "But at twenty-six, you're ready to marry? To take on a ready-made family? Because it's unnecessary. You can be part of our lives without becoming a husband and full-time dad. It's not what I expected from you when I came down here."

"But it's what you're getting." He crosses his arms in an obstinate gesture, and it feels like I'm arguing with a brick wall. A sexy lumberjack of a brick wall, but an uncompromising attitude won't get us far. All I'm trying to do is look out for the best interests of everyone—him included.

What makes you so sure your way—the slow, cautious way—is so much better?

I ignore the gibing thought, unwilling to admit to another major risk after the last one resulted in this situation. "We're not getting anywhere. Perhaps it'll be best to let the news settle before making a rash decision," I suggest, needing a breather. "Why don't we table this discussion for a later time? I've got to start driving back home, anyway." It's a long drive, and I already don't feel up for it as thoughts of getting a hotel for the night pop up.

You packed an overnight bag, "just in case", for a reason...

"Don't head back yet. Stay here, and we'll work on getting to know each other more. You can fill me in on what I've missed these past few months. Doctor's appointments, how you've been feeling, that kind of stuff."

It's sweet he cares so much, though it tears at the tenuous control I have to resist his persuading charm. Truly, I'd love to let him have his way, but what twenty-six-year-old man wants to settle down permanently so quickly?

He's being brash because the baby bomb is an all-encompassing shock wave. Once his senses have returned to normal, he'll regret offering marriage. And I don't think my poor heart could take a retracted proposal, especially if I'd agreed to it.

No, I need to protect all of us.

I need to keep a clear head and figure out a way to make him see reason.

He can be in our lives. We can co-parent. But we don't need to jump to permanent—or at least, legally binding—promises of forever.

Even if I secretly hope to hear those very promises from his lips and know without a doubt, *he meant them*.

CHAPTER SIX

MICAH

"I don't think that's a good idea..." A frown of doubt brackets her mouth, and fear slicks down my spine at letting her leave without a concrete plan for us being together.

"Come on, you'll love a night in the mountains, especially a fall evening where the stars are bright—shining crystal clear upon the lake," I cajole, pressing the advantage of our location.

She wants to wait to discuss the future? Fine. But we're sure as hell going to become friends. The first step is to get her to sleep over, so she can experience what living here with me would be like.

It'd be fucking perfect if I have my way.

"Micah..." Her decision's wavering, an exasperated huff filling the room while a reluctant grin toys with her pretty mouth. She's tempted; captive eyes sneak longing peeks out the windows lining the front of the house. It's beautiful, with the mountains as a backdrop to a freshwater lake and hundreds of evergreens.

Raising my right hand, I act as if I'm reciting vows in front of a judge. "I promise not to push the marriage thing and to keep my hands to myself... unless otherwise notified." My brows wiggle in the caricature of a lecherous expression—gunning for a full-blown smile from Kate and an acceptance of my invitation.

Part one of the mission accomplished.

I suppress a victorious pump of my fist when I catch the shy tilting of her lips and a faint giggle spills out. *God, I love when she laughs at my jokes.* I know I can be goofy and too much—if one listens to my brother—but Kate never seems to mind. In fact, I get the distinct impression that she's into my particular brand of charm—which is good, considering I'm definitely into everything about her.

"If I agree, where exactly am I going to sleep? Because as cute as a tiny home is, it doesn't leave much room for overnight guests."

Point taken.

"You'll use my bed in the loft while I sleep down here. Although, maybe you shouldn't be climbing the ladder to the loft in your condition..." I glance between her burgeoning belly and the slim ladder leading to the second level. Damn, I wasn't thinking straight when I decided to live in a tiny home. It's good enough for the bachelor I used to be, but terrible for a man with a family—the man I want Kate to let me be.

"Ladders are fine; I'm not an invalid." She stands and stretches, causing her shirt to ride up, giving me an enticing flash of the endearing bump housing our baby. All I want to do is hold it protectively in my hands, whispering all the words of hope and love sprouting inside me for the child and its mother. "Besides, I've always wanted to know what it was like living in a tiny home even for a brief moment, so this will be a fun adventure. There's a traveling bag outside that I brought in case I decided to drive home tomorrow. I'll grab it and—"

"No, I'll grab it." Pointing back towards her seat, I order, "You settle in here; think about what you want for dinner."

"Are you offering to cook?"

"You didn't think I lived on the side of a mountain without an essential survival skill, did you?" In truth, it took me years to buckle down and finally learn how to create a proper meal for myself, preferring the convenience of driving into town whenever I wanted to eat. But what Kate doesn't know won't hurt her. Besides, I like the look of admiration on her face at the discovery of my culinary talents.

That's right, little mama. I can cook, make you laugh, and fuck you to half a dozen orgasms. Just say the word.

"Good grief, don't look so pleased with yourself," she mutters, playfully shoving at my arm before plopping back into her seat. "It was just a question... though, is it really dangerous living up here?"

"We've had our fair share of power outages because of storms, but nothing too terrible. Don't worry; our new cabin will withstand anything Mother Nature throws at it." Maybe I should've kept that particular piece of information bottled for another time, but I don't want her thinking I can't provide what she needs.

"Our new cabin?"

"I promised not to talk about the future tonight, remember? That's all you're getting from me. For now." A mutinous expression crosses her adorable face, but she bites her lip in refrain. Whistling in amusement, I head outside to her car after grabbing the keys she tossed on the table, leaving her to mull over my words.

With a couple of phone calls, our new home will be well underway to be built in time for next spring, possibly around the time of her due date. And we can keep the tiny house as a small getaway for the two of us. The road ahead appears so obvious—a happily ever-after I never expected—if only Kate agrees to trust me and what we can build together.

CRACKLING FROM THE firepit snaps between us as I return to the Adirondack chair next to Kate's after a dinner of chicken alfredo. Time passed easily once we agreed to push the storm cloud representing our future to another day, and it felt natural to chat and tease, as if we've known each other forever.

"Are you warm enough?" She's huddled under one wool blanket already, but another chill wind blows past us, causing me to worry.

"I'm fine. Between my coat, this blanket, and the fire, I'm as toasty as can be." The bunched muscles in my shoulders relax, releasing the energy gathered to make a run inside. Rhett would laugh in disbelief at how overeager I am to assuage her every need. I haven't been an asshole to women in the past, but there was definitely more of a distance—an independence because this driving force to please and protect never existed before Kate.

Owl hoots emerge from the forest, and for the first time in months, contentment seeps into my bones. I spent most nights enjoying the calming sounds of nature—a familiar symphony—yet their lullaby had lacked its usual power until now. With Kate.

A peaceful silence blankets us until I break it with a random question as my mind relives our first night together. "What was your friend's wedding emergency?" The fateful phone call had ended our evening prematurely, and without it, who knows where we'd be now? Perhaps we would've stayed in touch.

"Oh, I'm surprised you remember." Kate laughs and tucks a stray strand of hair behind her ear.

I remember everything about that night. Cheesy but true.

"She was worried about her dress not fitting, then it spiraled into a bad omen meaning she shouldn't marry her fiance. It was something dumb, but you know how brides can be."

"Yeah, I've heard the horror stories." Gossip about bridezillas was hard to miss. "So, the wedding went on without a hitch?"

"I wouldn't say that." A cute giggle erupts. "Another bridesmaid fell twice walking down the aisle and ended up needing to leave early because her ankle was swollen and purple. I shouldn't laugh, but it was so unexpected. And for her to fall not once but twice!"

I chuckle along with her, envisioning the guests' reactions to the poor bridesmaid's fall—shock and nervous laughter, I'm sure. Observing Kate, my mind wanders to a different wedding, one where she's in white, and I'm the grateful groom waiting to call her mine forever.

"Speaking of weddings, it occurs to me that while you've got an inkling about my relational past, I have no idea about yours." Broaching a topic I've spent too much time contemplating cracks the relaxing atmosphere, but curiosity won't stop nipping at me. "What's the story? Because it surprises me how you can still be single."

A rueful chuckle precedes a muffled hum of sadness, and I wonder what she'll tell me. Has she already been married? Is that why she's hesitant with me? A million scenarios flash through my mind as I wait for her answer, fearing she might tell me she's already met and lost the love of her life and has nothing left for me.

Which would suck, but as pathetic as it might be, I'd take her however I can. I'll love her enough for the both of us. *Love*. What a funny notion: the charming serial dater is ready for commitment... but it's true.

"Not much to tell except for the five-year relationship I ended last year."

Fuck. That's a long time to be with someone. Did she still have feelings for this guy? Was she wishing he was the father of our child instead of me?

This feeling of uncertainty—insecurity—was new. As cocky as it sounds, usually I was the one who held the power in past relationships. Women flocked to me without much effort on my part. But hearing about Kate's ex, a relationship that spanned years, knocked me down a bit. How could I compare?

"He didn't want kids or marriage. He was happy with what we had, which included a long-distance relationship where we hardly saw one another. We were more like friends than lovers." She shrugs and snuggles deeper under the blanket before shooting a pleading look my way. "Is it any wonder I have a difficult time believing you're ready for marriage and a baby after knowing me for less than twenty-four hours? Even my boyfriend refused to commit to more after five years!"

"I'm not him."

Kate sighs, head tilting backward to stare at the stars above, resignation written in her drooped shoulders. "I know. Both of you are as different as can be, but it's difficult to believe I magically lucked into what I've wanted for years: a child, a husband. A family."

"Imagine what it's like for me. One moment I'm a perpetual bachelor—happy living for the moment. Next I meet a sexy brunette with curves for days, and I'm hooked. Ready for a forever kind of relationship."

"Yeah, that doesn't make me feel better about your decision-making skills." A teasing laugh softens the barb, and her lightened mood eases the tension in the air.

Leaning forward, elbows resting on my knees, understanding for her plight swirls in my gut, but it's not enough for me to let this go. To give her more time. Because I'm afraid she'll talk herself out of what she really wants—us raising a family together.

"Listen, I don't expect you to trust me one hundred percent right now. I don't expect you to feel as confident as I am in what we could have. All I want is for you to give us a chance; don't shut us down before we even get started." Debating my choices, I decide to offer a compromise, praying she'll accept it. "Agree to my proposal, but it won't mean we marry tomorrow or next week. As long as it's before the baby is born, months from now, I'll be happy."

She studies my expression, and I hope she reads the sincerity in my eyes. "I thought you agreed not to mention the future tonight." The throwaway comment's spoken without heat before she continues, "But I'll think about it. I suppose if it comes to it, a broken engagement is better than a divorce."

Relief cools the rising tide of worry... for now, at least.

"Thank you, that's all I ask."

MY MORNING WOOD WAKES me from a dream featuring Kate taking hold of my hard cock. Sunlight beams through the massive windows, and I hold my breath, waiting to hear if Kate's awake yet.

When nothing breaks the chirping of birds winging around outside, I chance a hand down my boxer briefs to trim the edge of my desire. Stroking my cock, I imagine Kate on her knees—bare to me—pink lips surrounding the mushroom head of my erection. Sweet suckling sounds resound in my head as she takes her time loving the tip, and my hand tightens reflexively.

That's it, baby. Just like that. I encourage dream Kate, wishing to hell she was really in bed with me. All those warm curves blanketing my body, the wariness in her eyes morphing into feverish need.

Yanking roughly on my dick, the fantasy intensifies as her delicate hand cups the hanging sac underneath, tentatively rolling it in her palm. A muted grunt of gratification stutters in my throat, and before long, spurts of cum drip down my length, soaking my hand and briefs.

I lay replete in satisfaction until rustling from above alerts me to Kate's waking presence. Tossing away my flannel blanket, I make quick work of cleaning up before she comes down.

The day ahead looms large and momentous. Kate's driving home, and I don't plan on letting her go alone, which will be sure to strike an argument. But it's imperative to prove my intentions, especially after she agreed to think about my compromise last night. Evidence of her resolve softening.

While I don't want to bully her into a decision, I get the sense she needs the nudging or else fear and doubt due to her past will rule.

Don't worry, little mama. You'll have what you need from me... I won't let you or our baby down.

CHAPTER SEVEN

KATE

"You didn't need to follow me home, you know. I drove to High Ridge alone yesterday, which means I'm capable of making the return trip just fine."

Micah's insistence on tailing me for the entire two and half hour drive back to my apartment was sweet and confusing and frustrating. He only wants to talk about being together more, and I can't handle that conversation anymore. The past twenty-four hours, my mind's been circling the subject non-stop, trying to figure out a way to consent to his proposal. To let go of my fear and accept what my treacherous, illogical heart wants.

Our discussion over the bonfire *did* ease some of my concerns. *He's ridiculously persuasive, knowing the right things to say.* A subdued smile glints back at me as I glimpse myself in the hallway mirror of my apartment.

But I hate that the impetus for all of this is my pregnancy. I don't want him to be with me just because we're having a baby. I want him to be with me because he wants me—pregnant or not—plain and simple.

He does want you. He's as much as said so already.

However, the protective walls erected around me refuse to lower and believe it's anything more than a passing fancy. *Stupid insecurities.*

"Sorry, little mama, but from now on, I'm sticking to you like glue. Get used to it. Since I missed out on the first four months of your pregnancy, I've got some time to make up for."

Rolling my eyes, I huff in annoyance, though I'm secretly pleased at his persistence. *God, make up your mind already!* These damn hormones will be the death of me, I swear. One second I'm willing to forget common sense and let him do what he wants, gambling on the truth of fairy tale endings. Then the next minute, I'm irritated with his refusal to listen, his determination to force a romantic relationship because of the baby.

"Fine. Do what you want," I mutter, tired from the long drive and needing a nap. There's science promoting the brain's power to solve difficult problems in dreams, right? Maybe this particular issue could be one of them. *Didn't work last night, did it?*

"No holds barred?"

My steps pause before reaching my bedroom. What an odd question, and when I say so, he holds up a pink vibrator, one that had been left standing tall and proud on the coffee table. Mortification pinkens my cheeks at the sight. I live alone, and lately, I've been super horny, so sue me for leaving a sex toy out in the open after watching Jamie Fraser in *Outlander*.

But it's not something I wanted Micah to find.

"Give it to me." I hold a hand out. "You're not supposed to see that."

Raising an arm above his head, he wags the toy in the air, the jelly butterfly on its side swinging with the movement. "Oh, I'm going to give it to you alright." The suggestive promise sends unexpected heat through my body, along with a wave of amusement.

"That sounds like a bad porno line. Stop playing around and hand it over."

"No," he refuses, stalking towards me. "You look tense, and I have just the thing to mellow you out."

"What are you talking about?" An uncontrollable quaver entered my voice before vibrating downward.

"Three things." His fingers quickly tick off the short list. "Take off your pants, lay down on the couch, and spread those gorgeous thighs. Because I'm about to help you release all that tension you're holding in. It can't be good for you or the baby."

This man is out of his mind, yet I must be, too, because I adhere to his commands without another protest. He's right; I need a release. It's been too long since I've felt his touch, and my former exhaustion transforms into undeniable heat prickling along raw nerves.

Rough fabric chafes the backs of my legs after I lower to the couch, feeling awkward and self-conscious all of a sudden. My body's changed since he last saw me, then I realize he never actually *did* see me. We fucked in a dark alley with our clothes on. Reaching a staying hand towards him, alarm begins to take hold. "Maybe we shouldn't. We've still got a lot to figure out, and sleeping together will cloud our judgment."

"I think yours could stand a little clouding." Micah bends down, arms encasing my sides, while his mouth brushes a comforting kiss over my forehead. "So far, all your judgment's gotten you are months of doing this alone. Days and nights dealing with the trials of growing a baby without the help of the man who'd love to be there for you."

The tight knot weighing in my heart loosens at his words, at his persistence. Could I really be this lucky? My doubtful statement from yesterday echoes again.

It didn't seem possible. Not for a woman like me who's spent the past five years with a boyfriend unwilling to start a family, only now to discover a man, ready and willing—purely by chance.

"Won't you let me care for you, little mama?" The whispered endearment tickles my ear as he traces the thin shell with his tongue before drawing a feathery line down my neck. A hitched breath falls from my lips at the raspy touch of his beard along my collarbone, dipping lower and lower until it meets the top button of my blouse. "Won't you let me, sweet Kate?"

God help me, but yes, I will.

It's impossible to resist him when he's giving tender caresses and soft words of encouragement. My body yearns for his—as does my stupid romantic heart. "For now," I allow, holding his gaze as nimble fingers work open a trail of buttons.

Another concession on your part. First, staying over at his place and now letting him fuck you again.

Micah pauses and tugs me forward a little. "And after?"

I don't answer, letting him read the reminder of our earlier discussion in the unspoken words.

Clearly, he doesn't like what he sees on my face because a determined frown firms his lips. "Guess I have my work cut out for me. But don't worry, darlin', I'm man enough for the challenge." His confidence sends a shudder of need straight to my pussy, while apprehension winds its way into my head. Micah's not like anyone I've ever met, and there's no doubt he's used to winning—a man with his looks and charm couldn't possibly ever lose.

What does that mean for me?

Surrender to him and enjoy his attention while you can.

Warm air wafts over my skin as he pulls my shirt off before dealing with the supportive bra underneath. Plain and beige, I wish I'd worn something sexier, but with heavy breasts, especially with this pregnancy, I need all the support I can get.

"I remember these beauties." Micah tweaks one nipple before licking around the raised flesh.

"Good to know they're memorable in your sea of women." A slight bite edges my tone, and I wince at the jab, remembering his brother's words at the lumberyard. "Sorry, that didn't come out right. We've all got pasts, and yours doesn't bother me..."

"It's alright. Rhett needs to learn when to keep his mouth shut. Something I'll remind him of when I next see him." Irritation wrinkles his brow, tempting me to smooth it with my finger.

Screw it.

Why should I hold back? I agreed to this moment, after all.

A hum of pleasure comes from Micah at the gesture, and a satisfied sense of rightness brings about my own. "Don't fight with your brother," I warn playfully. "He provided more insight into your life, although I can't say I'm surprised you have a prolific past with women. You've got a combination of lumberjack boy next door going on—a strangely potent mix."

"Lumberjack boy next door?" Micah laughs, head tilted back, exposing his muscular neck, and another urge to trace the masculine lines of his throat—to feel the physical vibration of his amusement—overtakes me.

"Trust me, it fits." The bristle of his beard tapers down to smooth skin as my fingertip maps the intriguing differences between us like the bump of his Adam's apple or the golden tan painted over firm muscles—nothing resembling my pale, fleshy body.

Winking with more of that boyish charm, Micah shrugs and catches my hand to place a swift kiss in the palm before returning to his previous pursuit: playing with my nipples. Which have grown incredibly sensitive with this pregnancy, evidenced by the yip of pain that jolts from me when Micah nips a bit too forcefully.

"Shit, did I hurt you?" He immediately pulls back in concern, and I force a calming breath.

"A little... You need to be gentler, since these hormones hype every nerve ending in my body." Wondering if I should address another potential issue, too, I continue with a sigh, cupping his cheek. "And while I adore the bearded look, even the scratchiness is pushing my limits at the moment. Sorry..."

"You don't have to apologize, little mama. I should've considered how careful I need to be now."

"Well, I'm not going to break or anything." A bubble of warmth encapsulates me in a cocoon of safety at his concern, though another part of me—the throbbing center focused on being filled by his cock—doesn't want him to hold back too much.

There are those conflicting emotions again...

"Maybe not, but I can still temper my lust enough to ensure your pleasure. It's the least I can do when you're carrying our child." Kneeling before me, vibrator in one hand while the other lifts my left leg until it hangs over the back of the couch, Micah gently urges me to lie down. "Now, close your eyes and relax. Let me do all the work for you." The heat of his large body covers mine before a wisp of humid air skims the delicate skin of my inner thigh.

Following his whispered instructions, my eyes shut, heightening my awareness of Micah's every move. The idea of relaxing, releasing the stress roped through my muscles, is too good to refuse. It's like a volcano of nerves has been building in my body the past few days. Even sleeping doesn't provide respite—my night in Micah's loft is a testament to the fact as I tossed and turned.

A wet path traces upward before his mouth brushes intimate curls. "I regretted not getting a taste of you the first time we were together; now's my time to rectify the mistake." Thumbs separating my folds, he slowly—painstakingly—sinks his tongue into my pussy, the contracting muscles eager to squeeze and caress the intruder.

Oh, my god. My ex hardly ever went down on me, preferring as little foreplay as possible. *Why did I stay with him for so long?*

Desperate hands cling to the back of Micah's head, tugging at the blonde locks. "Please, I need more..." He withdraws before pushing in again. The controlled pumping movement mimics an attempt to collect the final melted drops in an ice cream cone. Repeated in and out, purposely showing me how much he meant what he'd said—to taste, to savor, *me*.

"God, how are you so good at this?" The question rises unbidden in the sultry air.

Micah raises his head, a mischievous twinkle in his eyes, and I know a smartass comment is on the tip of his tongue. My hand shoots up to cover his slight grin. "Nevermind. Don't answer that."

"Whatever you say, little mama. It would've been too easy, anyway." We share an amused glance, and once again, the strange addition of humor to our lovemaking confuses me. It implies a certain level of comfort that goes beyond the physical. Suggests his faith that our connection is real and potentially long-lasting is true because I've never experienced such a thing with anyone else.

"And you're above cheap jokes?"

"Not usually, but for you, I'll make an exception."

I laugh. "How kind of you."

"Mhmm... Kindness is my middle name. Along with *charming*, *hilarious*, *excellent in bed*." He punctuates the last part with a press of a button, bringing my vibrator to life. "Speaking of which, is this sweet pussy ready for more?"

Licking my lips, eyeing the thick silicone with hunger, I moan in approval. *Hell, yes.*

"Perfect. Wouldn't want my girl feeling anything but pleasure." Micah draws the tip around my clit before letting its length rub between slick folds, dousing it in my cream. When he's satisfied with the amount of lubrication, he inches the vibrator deeper, breaching my opening until a sense of fullness stretches the tight muscles.

The heavy weight stills as the base bumps against me; Micah adjusts the fluttering butterfly until its two wobbling antennae sandwich my engorged clit. His name breathes out in a stuttered whisper at the concentrated sensation.

"Too much?" he asks, pulling the butterfly away, providing instant relief—and disappointment.

Head shaking back and forth, another groan passes my lips as he pumps the vibrator inside me, focusing on my G-spot. "I don't know... I can't think straight..."

"Then, we'll try again. If it starts to hurt, let me know, and I'll remove it." He replaces the antennae and adds his mouth, circling the gyrating silicone and my clit with his lips, sucking rhythmically to match the shallow thrusts of the vibrator. The dual sensations crash over me in waves of intense pleasure. I've never experienced anything like this before, and the intensity borders on excessive.

But I won't stop him.

I need to know what comes next, what it feels like to fall apart so completely, to surrender to a man so supremely. Seconds, minutes, pounding heartbeats later, the rush of adrenaline and endorphins explode and uncontrollable spasms wrack my body as my climax rips through me. A burst of continual pleasure that leaves me weak.

The earlier fatigue returns with a vengeance, though it's tinged with contentment as I float in a quiet state of bliss.

How wonderful if this could be my everyday life. All I'd need to do is trust Micah. To give in.

In the background, the persistent buzzing sound stops, and brawny arms wrap beneath my back and knees to carry me to my room. Sighing into Micah's chest, the tattoo of his rapid heartbeat drums against my cheek before he deposits me gently onto my bed. "Sleep, little mama. I'll be here when you wake."

And just like that I drift off to the first peaceful rest I've had in days.

CHAPTER EIGHT

MICAH

Once Kate's tucked into bed napping, I rummage through her medicine cabinets until I find a razor and shaving cream. They may not be meant for a man's beard, but they'll get the job done.

I don't have as thick of a beard as Asa or Rhett, more of a perpetual five o'clock shadow, but it'll be an adjustment being clean-shaven for the foreseeable future. Though it's not that much of a hardship. If it's too scratchy for my girl's sensitive skin, then it's got to go.

Remembering the berry pink nipples puckered for my attention, I adjust the quickly growing erection behind my jeans. Damn, she'd been sweet. *All over*, I thought, as the taste of her pussy lingers on my tongue. And soon she'd be even sweeter, with milk spilling from her tits. Greedy, depraved bastard I am, I can't wait to drink from her, to know such an intimate part of her.

Fucking hell.

My cock twitches imagining that day, and I try to dispel the growing arousal by focusing on the task at hand. Lathering the fruity-scented shaving cream on my cheeks and chin, the image of a young Santa Claus pops into my head before the razor shaves it away in careful strokes. When I'm done, I pat smooth cheeks with the dainty hand towel hanging from a sidebar and inspect my handiwork. *Not bad*.

Kate's bathroom continues the theme of homey signs from the rest of her apartment, the one hanging next to the mirror currently saying "Get Naked" in black cursive, and I snicker in delight at the sentiment.

Seasonal knick knacks lay sprinkled throughout the home as I exit the bathroom and take inventory. Pumpkins, woodland creatures, and various renditions of fall poems line the walls and shelves. Soon, they'll be decorating our home: the log cabin I'll start plans for once I'm back in High Ridge.

Checking in on Kate once more, I snag her keys to lock up behind me before buying packing supplies at the nearest store. She won't enjoy waking to a half-packed apartment, but actions speak louder than words.

I want her and the baby with me, not hours away. If that means taking aggressive action by preemptively boxing up her things, then so be it. Though, after this afternoon, I feel more positive about her changing attitude towards us. The strong pull between us obviously burns within her, too.

Now to take advantage of it.

Kate's mine. I lost her once due to hesitation and a misguided notion that what I felt couldn't possibly be as powerful as it was after one night. *Never again.* There's a connection between us that goes beyond the baby. Something that's been there since night one.

Box after box, I pack away Kate's living room. Maybe it's a dick move; I'm sure she's going to be pissed, but at least she'll realize how genuine I am.

Rhett mentioned my line of women, except the line ends here with her. There won't be anyone else for me besides Kate.

CHAPTER NINE

KATE

Stretching my arms overhead, a yawn escapes as I wake from my nap. Without stress and anxiety plaguing my dreams, I slept unencumbered for the first time in a while. The rejuvenating rest quells some of my nerves, granting me a reprieve.

The clock reads three o'clock, and I wonder what Micah's been up to all this time. I kind of wish he'd joined me in bed. Tearing myself from the comfortable bed with a yawn, I stumble out to the living room and see cardboard boxes stacked along a wall.

"What the hell?" Disbelief dispels the previous languor pervading my bones.

"Did you sleep well?" Micah asks from his position on the carpet, pulling books off of a bookshelf and filing them into a waiting box—acting completely normal. Like he's not overstepping his bounds.

"Are you serious right now? What are you doing? What is all this?" I wave a hand towards the systematic route he's clearly taken around the room, starting with the frames that used to hang on the wall by the couch to the bookshelf he's at now.

"I told you I want you to stay with me, and I meant it. I'm just helping you get a head start on packing."

"And you think manhandling my things will win points? Get me to agree to your proposition?" My hands flex on my hips as I resist stomping over to him, snatching the current book in his hand, and walloping him on the side of the head. "To think I was actually considering your proposal! Good to know I'd be signing up for a lifetime of overbearing behavior."

I ignore the glimmer of attraction to his barbaric move. *This isn't a romance novel; you can't let him alpha male you into submission.*

"I prefer protective behavior. Or helpful." He tries a boyish grin to lighten my mood, but it doesn't work. He can't charm his way out of this.

Are you sure about that?

"I have a life here, not in High Ridge. This news wasn't meant to compel you into some hasty shotgun wedding where we pretend we got married for anything other than the baby." Before he can protest, I rush forward. "Yes, there's attraction. Desire. But people don't build entire lives with those things as the foundation."

Why can't he understand?

Micah closes the cardboard box he's finished packing and sets it aside before standing to his feet. "I know. Which is why I'm offering you more time before officially marrying, but please don't ask me to live apart from you, too. I want to be there for you. For you both." He gestures to my rounded belly, and I rub the spot for comfort. To steady myself.

"I appreciate the sentiment. Truly, I do, but this kind of behavior?" I look around the half-packed room. "It's unacceptable. I won't be bullied."

"Understood. I'm sorry." Walking closer so only inches separate us, I can see the sincerity in his eyes. His quick apology rips the wind out of my sails. "This was a bad call on my part. I was hoping to prove my authenticity despite the ethics of the action; please don't shut me out because of one mistake."

Wavering, my hormones are firing all over the place—warring with my common sense.

Should I trust him?

Should I not?

Should I give us a chance?

Or not?

Where's a damned flower when you need one to make important life decisions? A slightly maniacal chortle threatens to erupt before I tamp it down. All those good, calming feelings from earlier are gone, and instead, a headache inches its way closer.

Do what you want even if it's the wrong decision, I tell myself. But the last time I listened, I ended up pregnant by a stranger.

Giving you the baby you've always wanted and possibly the man of your dreams.

It's hard to argue with that logic or to regret the wild decision I made at the bar that night. Maybe there's something to this taking risks thing after all.

Maybe instead of working myself into a lather of fear and doubt, I need to let go. These past four months have made me into a ball of nervous energy. An automaton intent on trying to control and prepare for every possible instance of failure or trouble.

I've spent long nights berating myself for my reckless decision that night at the bar, despite wanting this child with everything within me. Then it hits me.

Most of my trouble stems from the past and worrying about doing the right thing. Building a slow relationship. Keeping things at a snail's pace to ensure it's the correct path. But didn't I say I was tired of wasting time? Isn't that why I broke up with George?

My plan of waiting and seeing with him ended with me throwing away years of my life. I didn't deviate from the path until it was almost too late. Do I really want to make that error with Micah?

Undeniable terror unfurls in my gut at the prospect.

No, I don't.

I won't.

CHAPTER TEN

MICAH

Competing emotions flicker in her eyes, and genuine fear punches me in the gut. Was this one step too far? Did I finally push too hard?

"I don't want to shut you out," she finally says. "The truth is a part of me wants to give in to you, but it's difficult to ignore the reasons I shouldn't." Her fingers list a variety of problems. "You're young and used to playing the field. You say you want something permanent right now, but that can change in the blink of an eye. Not to mention, I don't want to be the only grown up in this relationship. I love how you can lighten a situation with your sense of humor, but when push comes to shove, are you capable of being an equal partner, to be serious?"

Time to throw a hail Mary.

Placing a pleading hand on Kate's arm, I pour my heart out to her, praying she listens and accepts my words as truth. "All right, here it is, heart on the line: I'm cheerful, easygoing, and sometimes irreverent. Not much gets me down." Kate stands frozen beneath my touch, eyes focused on me. "My brother cornered the market on grumpy and serious, but that doesn't mean that I'm irresponsible or can't take care of my woman and child. In fact, I think I'm uniquely qualified for those things, especially when it comes to you, little mama. You're the kind of woman who will keep our family grounded, something I've always needed even if I didn't always know it." Taking a deep breath, I continue, "But that doesn't mean I'm going to leave you hanging when you need me or force you into a role you don't want. If I'm not up to par yet, I'll get there; you can count on it. Say the word, and I'll do whatever you need for me to prove it."

"Okay."

One word.

And hope tentatively curls in my chest.

"I'll give you a chance, and we'll try it your way. Though I wonder if it isn't smarter for you to move here until we have a larger home, because your tiny house isn't going to work, especially as I get nearer the due date." Her hands glide over our protected baby in reflex. "Otherwise, we'll live together these next few months and see what happens. Maybe it'll end in marriage or we'll work out a co-parenting schedule if the romantic relationship doesn't work. Either way, I'm willing to take the leap of faith with you."

"That's all I'm asking for, darlin'."

We stand silent for a moment, letting the decision sink in. It's surreal that she's finally onboard and ready to trust me, and I've got an idea to seal the promise.

"Now that we're on the same page, how about we make it official?"

Wariness enters her gaze. "How?"

"I'm thinking you need another release after the stress of finding me out here rifling through your things, then you taking such a risk for me. Maybe you need a reward? Something to start this journey out, right?" I run a finger along her curves, from the apple of her cheek down the supple hill of her hip.

"Is this going to become a pattern? You easing my stress levels with sex?"

"Do you have a problem with it?"

"No, I don't think so." Her arms spread wide. "Have at it."

"It will be my pleasure."

My mouth crashes onto her, eager to taste my fill again. I amble backwards until the back of my knees meet the edge of the couch, and let us take a controlled tumble down. Her thighs brace either side of my hips as she grinds her pussy onto my rising cock.

"It seems the couch may become a habit, too." She giggles, but doesn't push to move to her bedroom. Honestly, we'll probably end up fucking on every available surface in this apartment if I have my way, so we'll get there, eventually.

All that matters to me now is showing my girl how ecstatic I am to call her mine. How pleased I am that she trusts me enough to take this risk.

I won't let her down.

Kate's mouth travels over my cheeks and down my neck, humming in surprise. "You shaved... It definitely makes you look younger without it." She bites a thick tendon before kissing the muscle and continuing. "But of course, you're just as attractive."

"Good to hear. Wouldn't want to disappoint you so soon after your decision to keep me."

Her mouth twists into a speculative smirk as she rocks against me, the action squeezing the breath from my lungs. "Is that what I agreed to? Are you going to be my *kept man*?" The teasing remark picks up the thread of our age differences, and my hips jerk up in response.

"Kept man. Baby daddy. General servicer of your needs. Call me what you want as long as it's *yours*."

Nuzzling into my throat, a purr of happiness rumbles from her, the soft sound reminiscent of a contented kitten, and I can't prolong this torture any longer. *I need to fucking pet her.* To caress and lick. Swallow each delectable drop of cream from her body.

Whipping her oversized tee off, I stared in awe at the naked wonderland in front of me. My mouth watered at her bountiful tits and rounded belly. *Am I developing a pregnancy kink?*

"You're so goddamned gorgeous," I mutter, seizing her breasts in a possessive hold. "I don't want you to ever cover up. You need to be on display all the time."

"Sounds cold." She jokes, though a flush of scarlet coats her skin at my praise.

"Don't worry. I'll be trailing your every move like a fucking fox on the hunt, ready to bend you over whatever's closest to warm you up real quick." Imagining taking her from behind—the peach of her ass arced for my touch—draws a drop of pre-cum from my cock.

We'll definitely be reenacting that scene.

"Hmm... my personal shadow prepared to fuck me at will?" Her hands tangle with the button of my jeans, eagerly skimming inside to pull my straining dick free. Licking her lips in an obscene gesture of hunger, Kate lowers her pussy to the bulging head, her heat scorching the thick stalk as she continues to sink down until I'm nestled to the hilt.

We both release groans of relief at finally being fully reconnected after all this time. Damn, I've missed this—missed her. Our one night together hadn't been enough, and neither will this. The certainty in my bones is concrete.

I'll need Kate for a long time. For the rest of our lives.

Murmuring enthusiastic words of devotion against her skin, I help her find a rhythm as she sways over me. It's a tantalizingly lazy pattern, meant to drive us to the finish line in a slow and easy fashion, instead of running headlong into climax.

Leaning forward, my mouth can't resist feasting on the undulating breasts that swing with each swirl of her hips. I latch onto a red nipple, trying to remember to suck tenderly, not savagely so as not to hurt her, when my control snaps at the honeyed beads of milk easing onto my tongue.

A growl of brutal possession rises in my chest, and I drag her nipple and the sweet nectar deeper, my cock swelling larger as she rides me.

"Micah... what..." Kate strains for coherency, her hands crushing me to her chest. "Don't stop..." The pliant muscles of her cunt choke my dick, and the trembling onset of her orgasm trigger my own.

Rough, convulsive lunges bury my cock deep as hot jets of cum coat her pulsing walls, a piercing cry drifting in the air as Kate succumbs to the cresting pleasure.

Gradually, we come down from the high, weak and spent, though I can't refrain from suckling her breast, unable to extricate myself from her sweetness. Quiet mewls of contentment reverberate between us: her drowning in a sea of bliss while I get drunk on her.

"I'd heard this could happen—producing milk as early as fourteen weeks. But I didn't think it'd happen to me." She manages to whisper the words into my ear, cuddling into me.

"Thank god, it did. Means I don't have to share yet." Not that I'd ever mind our baby its rightful due to its mother's milk, but the primitive part of me revels in owning this element of Kate without another's claim.

"God, you're greedy." But she doesn't seem to mind as her hips twitch against mine like she's ready to go another round.

"Mmm... I think you are, too, little mama. Good thing I've got the stamina to match you toe to toe."

"You think?" Kate intentionally tightens her pussy around my thickening cock and winks. "We'll see about that."

Goddamn.

Yes, we will.

EPILOGUE ONE

MICAH
ONE YEAR LATER

"There's my girl." I pick up my cooing daughter who looks adorable as fuck in her little elf outfit, knitted cap, and boots that Kate made for her.

McKayla Katherine Olson. My sweet baby girl.

She's perfect, like her mother, with dark hair and bright eyes, and I can't get enough of her.

"Don't get her too riled before we have to leave. I want her to have enough energy for the photoshoot," Kate warns from the master suite. We finished our cabin in record time, and we were able to move in two weeks before McKayla was born. She'll always know this as home, and I couldn't be happier.

"Don't worry; she'll be fine. Won't you, baby?" I tickle McKayla under her chubby chin until she releases a sweet coo of pleasure. Today we're shooting our family photo for Christmas cards, since Kate's always one step ahead of schedule. She prefers having everything checked off her list of to-dos months in advance if possible.

The guiding light of our family, my wife, is nothing if not reliable and steadfast—on top of being deliciously sexy. A flashback to last night reminds me of exactly how delectable she is when I picture how she looked riding my tongue in the shower. One leg slung over my shoulder as she ground herself against me.

Mmm... I'm tempted to put McKayla down for a quick encore, but I know Kate's determined for everything to go off without a hitch. Especially since it's not only our little trio being photographed. Somehow, she banded together with Asa and Rhett's women to form a massive holiday photoshoot extravaganza. It's sure to be chaotic.

And I wouldn't have it any other way.

Snagging Kate by the hips when she nears, I kiss her forehead and whisper, "I love you, darlin'," unable to resist voicing the words I adore telling her.

Blushing, something I find incredibly sweet after all these months, she playfully pats my cheek. "I love you, too, though don't think it'll get you off the hook if McKayla decides to sleep the entire photoshoot because of you." She softens the warning with a gentle peck below my ear before wriggling away.

"You hear that, sweetheart? Don't get daddy in trouble with mama. We want to see your pretty smile today." McKayla grins up at me in agreement, tightening the grip she has on my heart.

The clasp both she and her mama have.

The two girls I claimed after a one-night affair...

And I'd do it again.

EPILOGUE TWO

KATE

FIVE YEARS LATER

Pulsing lights illuminate the club floor, and I weave through groups of dancers, heading towards the bar. Stealing a free stool, I cozy up to the counter, allowing the short skirt of my dress to ride high on my thighs. A mischievous grin plays about my mouth as I contemplate the surrounding scene.

Electric sparks tingle along my spine as a pair of corded arms cage me against the sticky countertop. "Evening, darlin'. What's a sexy girl like you doing, sitting here all alone? Doesn't your man worry about someone else snatching you up?"

Breathless from Micah's graveled voice, I shrug, continuing our little role play. Every now and again, we enjoy getting out of the house and pretending it's the first night we met each other—horny strangers in a bar, who can't keep their hands to themselves.

"I wouldn't know. I've learned it's tough to find a man who's experienced enough to satisfy my... appetites," I tease as his hand courses over the bare skin of my thigh. "It's easier to keep to myself than to keep a man."

"Sounds like you've been meeting the wrong men." He nibbles the side of my neck, hot breath tickling my ear. "Why don't you let me show you how *right* I am? How I'll claim this cunt as mine and have you begging for more?"

Oh, my. He is in a mood tonight.

Thankfully, when the Neanderthal Micah peeks out to play, my favorite nights ensue.

"Right here?"

He grins as we recite the lines from our first meeting. "Wherever you want. It's your decision."

"I want you here. Now." *Always.*

Grabbing my hand, he drags me off the chair and paves a path outside. Warm air brushes over my heated body at the change of scenery.

Suddenly, Micah spins me forward until my back hits the brick wall of an alley, finishing the conversation with a proud rumble. "A woman after my own heart." Then his mouth bends to devour mine, and love bursts in my chest.

This man and our daughter are my life. A life that's anything but staid or boring, like I feared it would be. I've never regretted a single day since the choice I made to trust him and leap into the unknown.

And with his whispers of adoration panting into my skin, I know I never will.

Don't miss Rhett's story in Found by the Loner!

Grumpy Rhett is the last lone man on Black Mountain. His brother and best friend have both found the curvy women of their dreams, but he doubts love is in his future. Until a snowstorm sends a fallen angel his way...

As a body-positive influencer, Nora's learned how to embrace her curves. However, it's hard to believe anyone else will...especially the surly lumberjack who came to her rescue.

Will cabin fever ignite between this curvy girl and mountain man? Or will their fears and doubts melt away any chance at love?

Quick and steamy, this grumpy/sunshine duo is heating up the mountain one snowy night at a time!

THANKS FOR READING & DON'T FORGET TO RATE/ REVIEW!

Please consider leaving a rating/review on Amazon, Goodreads, Instagram, TikTok, and/or any other sites you review on.
Ratings & reviews are the #1 way to support an indie author like me.
They don't have to be long or even positive (though I hope you enjoyed this book!). All the algorithms care about are QUANTITY.
The more reviews, the more my books are shown to other potential readers!
And they serve as guides to readers on whether or not to take a chance on an indie author.
I appreciate your support!
XO, Hallie

ABOUT THE AUTHOR

Hallie prefers steamy, insta-love stories where curvy girls are claimed by filthy-talking heroes. And when she ran out of reading material, she decided to write her own stories. If you want a quick, hot read, she's your girl!